The Keep

MANDY COLEMAN

Illustrated by Brenda Cantell

sundance™
A Haights Cross Communications Company

The Characters

Mitchell

The knight

The king

The Story Setting

TABLE OF CONTENTS

CHAPTER ①

Board Games

Mitchell had never met anyone who loved board games as much as his family did. They had every board game ever invented.

Chess was now the game of the month.
His brother and father played chess almost
every night. Mitch often watched and
sometimes played, but he hardly ever won.

7

The large chessboard had tall, carved pieces on it. Mitch didn't know where the set was from, but he knew it was pretty old, older than his father.

The pawns had brave faces. They were tough little foot soldiers. Mitch liked how they stood up to any opponent, no matter how fierce. Mitch's favorite pieces were the bishops in their stately costumes. They always surprised their opponents. They were never direct, always unexpected.

As Mitch moved closer to the board, he saw the knights glance at one another. Then, to his surprise, Mitch heard the chinking sound of metal on metal and the loud snort of a knight's nervous horse. He could see the battle was about to begin.

The white bishop was unguarded. Mitchell watched as the black knight and his pawns gathered to charge. A shrill battle cry went up. Swords and shields crashed, followed by the final cry as the white bishop fell.

Mitchell's heart was pounding. This chess game seemed so terrible but also more amazing than ever before.

The white king was now in danger. His queen gave orders for the army to stand and defend. The battle cry sounded as the black knights led the charge.

The white queen and the castle were soon lost. Now, the powerful white king was looking scared. The pawns were too confused and weak to listen. The battle was lost.

As his brother knocked the last chess
pieces down, Mitchell heard their cries.
He looked at the mess on the battlefield.
His angry eyes filled with tears.

"How could you? They were so brave.
You've destroyed their kingdom! I hate
you, I hate you, you destroyer!"

"Mitchell," his father tried to soothe him. "It's just a game. Don't take it so badly."

"No! No! You don't understand. He's destroyed everything!" Mitchell cried as he ran to his bedroom. Lying on his bed, Mitchell's mind was whirling. He drifted into dreams of battles and soldiers, swords and armor.

CHAPTER 2

The Battlefield

The next morning it was all a blur. Did I imagine it? Or did it really happen? Mitch wondered. Last night's battle was clear and real in his mind.

Maybe . . . just maybe . . . I have the power to see into games. Wow! Cool! he thought.

This was great. What other games could
he try? Mitch looked around his room.
Toy soldiers were scattered on the floor.
His car collection and books were on the
bookshelves.

Then he saw just the thing on top of the bookcase. It was a battle game that had a battlefield to spread out on the floor.

"Yes! Yes! Yes!" he shouted.

This game was huge. It had knights, demons, and a king. If he could see into this game, it would be amazing. It would be great. He couldn't even imagine how cool it would be.

Mitch carried the game into the sunroom. With dreams of being a powerful knight leading his own army into battle, he unfolded the battlefield. Then he placed the plastic castle at the bottom of the mountain.

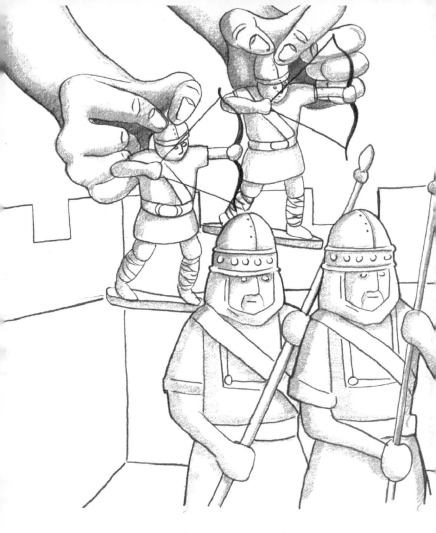

Quickly, he tipped the box of figures onto
the floor. He picked out a group of royal
guards and set them down in pairs.
Grabbing the archers, he put them in key
defensive positions.

When Mitch found the knights, a thrill went through him. He was so excited. He would be going into battle with these brave soldiers. Finally, he was going to find out how it all worked.

Next he placed the enemy. The Wolfriders, Pig-faced Thugs, and Orcs. The Orcs guarded the evil castle and its Keep, the jail. Mitch and his army were going to defeat these forces of evil.

Mitch and his brother had painted the Orcs. They had evil eyes and ugly faces. They had painted them with scars and warts, boils, and strange green splotches.

Everything was now in place. All he had
to do was grab a weapon. Mitch went
into his bedroom and grabbed his plastic
sword and helmet. He buckled his sword
over his pajamas and put on his helmet.

With a roll of the dice, he started the game. He moved the knights forward. Nothing happened. He rolled again and moved the Wolfriders. Their faces were still frozen in a plastic frown. Why wasn't anything happening?

How could he have been so stupid? Games don't come to life! It must have all been a dream.

Disappointed, he walked onto the plastic battlefield to pick up the castle. Suddenly, he felt a bolt of electricity run up through his feet. Everything went dim and icy cold. The sunroom started to break up and fly apart, and Mitch screamed.

He landed with a loud thud, facedown in thick mud. He lay sprawled in the mud, with dirt in his mouth and a heavy weight on his back.

"Now boy, are you going to get up?"

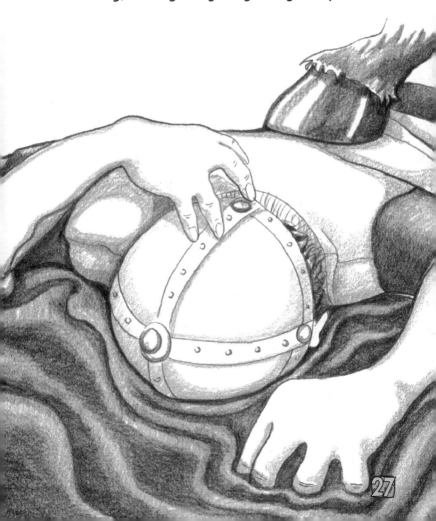

CHAPTER 3

The Castle

Mitch turned to look up into the face of a
knight. He'd thought that knights would
look like his father. But this knight was
fierce and frightening. Mitch knew he was
a knight only because of the pattern that
Mitch had painted on his shield.

"What are you doing, boy? You should be cleaning my weapons!" ordered the knight.

"But, but I um . . . ," Mitch stuttered.

29

As Mitch started to get up, a bloodcurdling growl came from the bushes. A huge, slobbering Orc came rushing toward them. The knight held firm as his horse reared up and squealed.

As the horse's hooves hit the ground, the knight lunged forward. His sword crashed down onto the Orc, and he and Mitch were covered with stinking, brown ooze.

"Come on, we'd better get out of here. Orcs never travel alone," boomed the knight as he dragged Mitchell up onto the saddle. They galloped down the mountain toward the castle.

Down in the valley, Mitch saw what must
have been his plastic castle. It had been
transformed into real stone. Its dark walls
rose high above them.

The knight paused and gazed up at the central tower. "See up there, boy? That's the Keep. That's the prison where they've got our king. I have to get up there and save him."

Mitch remembered that his brother had locked the king up weeks ago. He was still locked in the tower!

Mitch tried to remember who was where. He was sure he had placed two Orcs at each corner.

"There are two sentry Orcs on the north and west corners of the Keep!" he yelled out to the knight.

"But, of course," boomed the knight. "They are guarding the only entrances."

"No, there is another entrance," whispered Mitch urgently.

Long ago, Mitch had made a trapdoor at the southern corner of the castle. He had painted it to look like wood. Maybe he could find the trapdoor, get inside the castle, and help save the king. He knew this castle better than anybody!

As they galloped closer to the
castle, the horse pulled up suddenly,
and Mitch felt himself falling. He landed
in the bushes just outside the castle walls.

"Stay here and keep quiet," hissed the
knight as he charged off.

Scratched and bruised, Mitch scrambled out of the bushes. He picked up a branch and began hitting the stone wall. He needed to find that trapdoor.

The rock was solid and hard, but then he hit something softer. The trapdoor made a soft thud. It was solid wood. He traced its edges and found the catch. When he hit it with a branch, it sprung open.

Without a thought of the dangers inside,
he crawled into the castle. He had to find
his way to the Keep.

CHAPTER 4

Into the Dungeon

Mitch stood waiting for his eyes to adjust to the darkness of the tower. A stone staircase ran up to his left. Mitch knew it led to the Keep and to the king. He saw no guards, so he ran up the stairs.

The stairs seemed never ending, spiralling up
and up. His legs and lungs started to burn.

When Mitch reached the top, he was out of breath. He peered through the bars of the locked prison door. He saw a huge man shackled to the wall. This must be the king.

"Boy, you must get that key, over there, on the wall!" the king said.

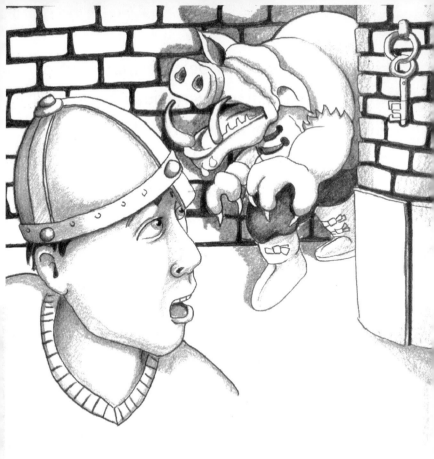

Reaching the key wasn't going to be easy.
As he turned, Mitch saw a Pig-faced Thug
slowly shuffling toward him.

Pig-faced Thugs are blind and slow but
extremely strong. They have powerful
claws and massive jaws.

Mitch didn't want to become this monster's next meal. Very quietly, he picked up a broken jug from the floor and threw it to the right of the Thug. It hit the wall with a loud crash, and the Thug turned toward the noise. Mitch ran to where the key hung on the wall.

"Quickly, boy!" the king yelled.

Mitch grabbed the key and ran to unlock
the prison door. The Thug was angry now.
It was coming toward Mitch, swiping at the
air with its razor-sharp claws. Mitch quickly
put the key in the lock and turned it.

As Mitch unlocked the king's shackles,
they clanged loudly. The Thug turned
toward the new sound.

"Down the stairs!" the king yelled.

Mitch ran for his life down the stairs.
The Pig-faced Thug was coming after
them, snarling and growling. Its heavy
footsteps were pounding down the stairs.

The king pulled Mitch through a door.
They were in a room full of weapons.

"Wait here!" said the king as he took up
a sword and ran back up the stairs.

Mitch heard the clash of metal. He knew
that the Pig-faced Thug was no match for
the powerful king. Still trembling, Mitch
looked around the room full of axes,
knives, spears, and hundreds of swords.
Mitch had never seen such large swords.
Some were taller than he was.

Mitch heard a bellow and a loud crash, and then the door flew open. The king ran through the room and leaped out the window. Mitchell raced to the window to see the king stab the last surviving Orc in its stinking heart.

Next to the Orc, the knight sat injured. He was slumped on the ground bleeding, but he was smiling at the king. Mitch couldn't believe it. He had saved the king!

With his heart pounding in his chest,
Mitch turned back to the weapons in the
room. A silver sword lay on the great
table, along with shields and daggers.
In one corner, Mitch saw an enormous
wooden chest. The treasure!

The lid of the chest was incredibly heavy. As Mitch heaved it up, he saw the most gorgeous jewels gleaming in the light from the window.

He touched the emeralds, diamonds, and
rubies, and then he saw it—a huge opal.
His mom's opal? It seemed to flicker and
burn. He could see blue flames inside the
opal. He reached out, and it was hot to
touch. The room began to spin and break
apart as Mitch was thrown to the ground.

CHAPTER 5

Back Home

This time he wasn't scared. Mitch felt himself falling, and he opened his eyes. He fell and fell through the swirling light.

He landed headfirst on the sunroom rug.
He opened his hand, and the opal was
still there. His mother's opal had brought
him back home.

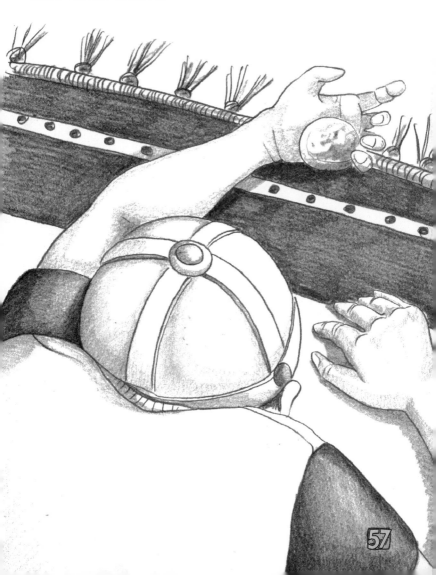

His mother walked into the room carrying
a tray of pancakes, juice, and honey.

"Oh Mom, you're a lifesaver," Mitch said as he rushed to hug her. She smiled until he got close to her.

"Mitchell, what is that all over you? You stink! What have you been doing?"

Mitch looked at his pajamas. They were covered with dirt and Orc's blood, but he didn't care. He had helped to save the king.

While Mitch ate his breakfast, he thought about the battle game. Would he ever go back? Maybe he could try a different game. He looked around the room and then his eyes came to rest on the computer. "I wonder . . ."

GLOSSARY

opponent

one on the opposite side

royal guards

the king's guards

shackled

tied in irons

slobbering
dribbling

sprawled
stretched out

stately
dignified

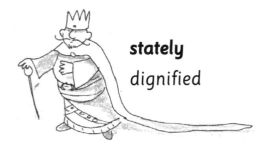

transformed
changed

Talking with the Author and the Illustrator

Mandy Coleman (author)

What did you want to be when you grew up?
A trick horse rider in a circus.

Which animal would you most like to be?
A dragon or a crusader's gallant steed.

Brenda Cantell (illustrator)

What did you want to be when you grew up?
Famous.

If there were only two colors in the world, what should they be?
Azure blue and gray-green.

Which animal would you most like to be?
An albatross. They can fly for thousands of miles across the sea without landing.

Published by Sundance Publishing
P.O. Box 1326, 234 Taylor Street, Littleton, MA 01460
800-343-8204
www.sundancepub.com

Copyright © text Mandy Coleman
Copyright © illustrations Brenda Cantell

First published 2000 as Sparklers by
Blake Education, Locked Bag 2022, Glebe 2037, Australia
Exclusive United States Distribution: Sundance Publishing

ISBN 0-7608-6973-1

sundance™
A Haights Cross Communications Company